CHASING
GEORGE WASHINGTON

CHASING
GEORGE WASHINGTON

★ By Ronald Kidd ★

Based on the musical play by Karen Zacarías and
Deborah Wicks La Puma with the young playwrights of
Young Playwrights Theater in Washington, D.C.

Commissioned by the John F. Kennedy Center for the
Performing Arts and the White House Historical Association

★ Illustrated by Ard Hoyt ★

SIMON & SCHUSTER BOOKS FOR YOUNG READERS
NEW YORK LONDON TORONTO SYDNEY

SIMON & SCHUSTER BOOKS FOR YOUNG READERS
An imprint of Simon & Schuster Children's Publishing Division
1230 Avenue of the Americas, New York, New York 10020

SIMON & SCHUSTER BOOKS FOR YOUNG READERS is a trademark of Simon & Schuster, Inc.
For information about special discounts for bulk purchases, please contact Simon & Schuster
Special Sales at 1-866-506-1949 or business@simonandschuster.com.
The Simon & Schuster Speakers Bureau can bring authors to your live event.
For more information or to book an event, contact the Simon & Schuster Speakers Bureau at
1-866-248-3049 or visit our website at www.simonspeakers.com.
Book design by Chloë Foglia
The text for this book is set in Bembo.
The illustrations for this book are rendered in pencil.
Manufactured in the United States of America
2 4 6 8 10 9 7 5 3 1
Library of Congress Cataloging-in-Publication Data
Kidd, Ronald.
Chasing George Washington / by Ronald Kidd ; adapted from a play by
Karen Zacarías and Deborah Wicks La Puma with the young playwrights
of Young Playwrights Theater; illustrated by Ard Hoyt.—1st ed.
p. cm.—(The Kennedy Center presents: Capital kids)
"Commissioned by the Kennedy Center and the
White House Historical Association."
Summary: When three students, feeling out of place during a White
House tour, bump into a painting of George Washington, the president
comes to life and leads them on an insider's tour, during which they
meet many former residents.
ISBN 978-1-4169-4858-2
ISBN 978-1-4169-9710-8 (eBook)
[1. White House (Washington, D.C.)—Fiction. 2. Washington, George,
1732–1799—Fiction. 3. Presidents—Fiction.
4. Presidents—Family—Fiction. 5. United States—History—Fiction.]
I. Zacarías, Karen. II. La Puma, Deborah Wicks. III. Hoyt, Ard, ill. IV. Title.
PZ7.K5315Ch 2009
[Fic]—dc22
2009009013

FIRST
EDITION

★ ★ ★ CONTENTS ★ ★ ★

FROM THE DESK OF

★ ★ ★ MICHELLE OBAMA ★ ★ ★

For anyone who has only seen the White House on television, or visited it on a school trip—as the children in this story did—the home of the presidents can seem like a very formal and proper place. The precious antiques, formal portraits, Tiffany stained glass and Italian marble mantels can make you feel like you're in a museum instead of a home.

"We don't belong here," say the children in the story. It's easy to see how someone could feel that way. My family and I were very excited about moving into this house filled with history, and a little bit nervous about so many breakable things! But we learned, as Annie, Dee, and José learn in the course of the story, that while this house is filled with history, it is also filled with family memories.

In this magical book, three present-day kids from different backgrounds get a very unusual tour of the White House from George Washington himself. With President Washington, they travel back in time (just steps ahead of the secret service man who's hot on their heels and determined to return them to their school group). They meet the Lincoln children, who shared the White House with Union soldiers in the Civil War. They watch Caroline Kennedy play hide-and-seek. They chat with Susan Ford, who had her high school prom in the East Room—but also did chores every day and her homework every night, just as Malia and Sasha do.

Most importantly, Annie, Dee, and José learn that they *do* belong in the White House, because this house belongs to everyone. It's the people's house. The story of the White House is the story of our country, and the best thing about our country is that everyone belongs.

Even though more than a million people tour the White House every year, many Americans will never have the opportunity to visit. I hope that you will visit someday, but until then, this book can open the doors of the White House to you in ways that even a personal tour never could. That's what books do: They show us new worlds, reveal our history, and open our eyes to new ways of seeing things. I'm glad you're sharing this White House adventure with us, and I wish you many more adventures in reading!

Sincerely,

Michelle Obama

THE PRESIDENT'S SHOES

★ ★ ★ DEE ★ ★ ★

No cell phones?

It had to be some kind of joke. I mean, my cell phone is like my second mouth. Or my third ear. Or my fourth nostril. Okay, that's random, but you get the idea. I need my cell phone. And she was telling me I couldn't use it?

She was short and chunky—my mom would say "full figured"—and when she talked, she sounded like a textbook. I am not kidding. Can you say boring? She was in charge of our tour group, which meant we were stuck with her for the next couple of hours. She had told us to call her Ms. Letter. Excuse me? That's not a name. It's a school supply.

No cell phones? What planet was she from? What

kind of place was this, anyway? What had I gotten myself into?

I'm Diana, from the cool town of Hotlanta, Georgia. But you can call me Dee-Dee, or Dee. You can also call me Dimples, Lady Dee, or Diamond.

I live in the suburbs in a brand-new house with a brand-new yard. And since my dad's promotion, we got a brand-new car and stopped mowing our brand-new lawn. My dad says he spent his youth mowing lawns, and he is never doing it again. So we pay for a fancy service to cut our grass every week.

We have four bathrooms, and one of them is mine. I'm an only child, which is great because I have my very own everything. If I haven't mentioned it yet, I'll tell you now. It rocks to be me!

Anyway, Ms. Letter was in charge of the tour, and she said no cell phones. She also said . . . well, I'll let you hear for yourself.

"Before we begin this most exciting adventure," she droned, "we need to go over some rules. Be aware of the exits. No food or drink. Do not chew gum or eat candy. All right? Good.

"Now, I'm Ms. Letter, and it is my pleasure to welcome and congratulate you for being here today. You've worked hard, and so you have been selected to come to Washington DC to tour parts of the White House where most people are not allowed. Yes, you are the 'Children of Today' learning the history of yesterday for the future of tomorrow. And I am so excited."

Suddenly she stopped and clapped her hands. "Pop quiz!"

I groaned. We got enough of those in school.

"We are in one of the most famous places in the world!" she said. "What is the street address?"

Looking around the group, she pointed to a boy in the back. He had dark eyes, and his pants hung low. I think maybe she picked him because she didn't think he would know the answer.

He looked up at her and grinned. "It's 1600 Pennsylvania Avenue."

She gazed at him, surprised. "And this house at 1600 Pennsylvania Avenue—what is it called?"

"It's the White House, huh!" He spun around, did the splits, and came up smiling.

"That's very . . . expressive," said Ms. Letter.

Okay, the guy was different, but he was also kind of interesting. "Who are you?" I asked him.

He said, "Listen up, okay? And look this way, 'cause I am José from LA. And today, we're going to play, and see the White House. Oh-heyyy!"

"Are you weird?" I asked him.

"No, I'm José!"

Ms. Letter watched him nervously. I think she was afraid she might be losing control of the group. "Children of today," she said, "who ordered the White House built?"

A girl in front raised her hand. Her blond hair was woven into a braid, and she carried a guidebook and a little notebook that she scribbled in. Speaking with an accent, she put her words together in an unusual way.

"The president, General George Washington, picked design . . . but died before its completion. He is only president who did not live in White House. I read this in book. I write it in my notebook."

"Very good," said Ms. Letter. "And you are?"

"I am Anita Alicja Kalinowska. Or Annie. I am coming from Kansas City."

Listening to her accent, José shook his head. "Dude, you are not really from Kansas."

Annie smiled. "You right!"

"I knew it!" said José.

"I from Missouri," she said. "That where my Kansas City located."

Ms. Letter clapped her hands. "And now, children, the big moment has arrived. It's time to begin our tour! Line up, please. Two neat rows."

Rows? If I had wanted rows, I would have joined the marching band.

We lined up, and she led us down a hall. As we walked, she talked. "Tell me, children, what does the White House mean to you. Anybody?"

I said, "The fancy home of the president?"

Annie said, "A historical museum."

José said, "An excuse to miss class!"

Ms. Letter sighed, and we kept walking. We went by a bedroom, and I tried to peek inside. The president is a regular person, right? He has a house. He has a cell phone. I wondered if he liked shopping for shoes.

I raised my hand. "Will we get to see the president's shoes?"

"No," said Ms. Letter.

"Can we read the books in library?" asked Annie.

"No," said Ms. Letter.

José said, "Will we get to see top secret documents?"

"No!" said Ms. Letter.

"Then what *will* we see?" I asked.

"Furniture!" she said. "Antique furniture."

They call them antiques, but really it just means old. The house was old. Ms. Letter was old. Looking around, I was starting to feel old too.

And I was getting older by the minute.

CHiLL, DUDE

★ ★ ★ JOSÉ ★ ★ ★

Check it out, man. The White House, home of the president—número uno, top gun, the big kahuna.

The truth? When they told me I was going to the White House, I got all excited. But it wasn't because of the house. It was the trip—my first time on a plane. Plus, I'd be getting out of math class.

When the plane landed, I looked around and thought, Hey, this is all right. I'm in Washington D.C. Lots of cool people there. Like El Señor Presidente. Maybe I'll see him on this tour—you know, working at his desk or grabbing a snack or watching a giant flat-screen TV.

"Hey, Mr. President," I'd say. "What's up, man? How's

it going? You need help from somebody with slick moves and lots of style?"

He'd look me up and down, taking it all in. Maybe I'd give him a demo. Move number 33–B. The helicopter. Stand back, okay? It's a little tricky. Kids, don't try this at home.

"Young man!"

Huh?

"Young man, I'm speaking to you."

I looked up. It was our tour guide, Ms. Letter.

"May I ask what you're doing?" she asked.

"The helicopter," I said.

"Well, shut it off. Turn in your rotors. We don't want to break the dishes."

She walked over to a fancy wooden cabinet. "Children of today, I've got something exciting to show you— dishes from China! Look, but don't touch." She glanced at me. "And whatever you do, don't dance!"

Don't dance?

You might as well ask that dude Picasso not to paint. Or LeBron James to quit playing basketball. Dancing? It's what I do.

Did I mention my name? It's José. And don't forget the accent over the *e*.

I live in LA., in an apartment above the car wash that

my family owns. If you look out my bedroom window, you can see the fire station and Frankie Fried Chicken, and if the smog's not too bad you can spot the tip of the *d* in the Hollywood sign. Our place is small but cool and very, very clean.

I live with my mom, my brother, my aunt, and my uncle, at least until my aunt has her baby. One of us is always in the kitchen, looking for leftovers. We usually find them too. My family may not have as big a house as the president, but I bet we have better food. Better tortillas for sure.

Ms. Letter closed the cabinet door and led us around the room, pointing things out. "The White House has beautiful objects from all over the world: Italian marble mantels, Turkish sofas, English carpets . . ."

I said, "Hey, man, I don't get it. Is this a house or a museum?"

"It's both!"

She took us down a long hallway, and we followed. Well, most of us did. I ducked into a side room—you know, figuring I'd have a little tour of my own.

Everything was going fine. I was checking out a closet the size of our car wash, when all of a sudden I felt a hand on the back of my neck. The hand swung me around, like I was a doll in a puppet show. The hand was connected to a big dude in a suit.

"What do you think you're doing?" he growled.

"Hey, watch it!" I said. "I need that neck."

The dude said, "No looking around. No freelancing. Stay with your group."

He marched me down the hall and back to the tour. Some of the kids giggled when they saw me. Ms. Letter didn't think it was so funny.

"Let this be a lesson to all of you," she told the group. "Don't wander off. If you do, you'll have to deal with Mr. Flower."

I smiled at the dude. "Flower? That's your name?"

"Yeah. Want to make something of it?"

"Hey, I saw you in a movie," I told him.

"Movie?"

"Let's see," I said, "what was the name of it? Oh, yeah. *Bambi*."

He gave me a death stare.

"Oops," I said. "Wrong guy."

Ms. Letter stepped to the front of the group. "I'm glad you're here, Mr. Flower. Maybe you could review the rules and tell the children some facts about the White House."

Nodding, he hooked his thumbs over his belt. "Okay, listen up! No gum, no food, no drinks, no fuss, no flash, no cell . . ."

He glared at a girl named Dee, who was doing a quick text on her cell phone. She closed the phone and said, "This is so unfair."

Mr. Flower went on. "Don't touch, don't sit, don't push, don't lean, don't scratch, don't itch . . ."

Another girl raised her hand. Her name was Annie. I liked the way she talked. It was different, almost like music.

"You tell us all the many things we can't do," she said. "What *can* we do?"

"Enjoy your stay," he said.

★ || ★

Mr. Flower led us down the stairs and into the kitchen. It was huge! My mom would have loved it, man. She could make mole verde for everybody in LA, plus a few extras.

"With five full-time chefs," said Mr. Flower, "the White House kitchen is able to serve dinner to one hundred forty guests, and appetizers to more than a thousand."

"Which basically is like feeding an *army*!" said Ms. Letter.

"Appetizers?" I said. "Cool! Like those itty bitty hot dogs? I love those."

Annie said, "My mother make good sausage."

Dee turned up her nose. "I prefer sushi."

Hearing our comments, Mr. Flower had been fidgeting impatiently. Finally he couldn't stand it anymore.

"*Attention!*" he yelled. "You're supposed to listen, not talk!"

We stared at him. His face was all red.

"Mr. Flower," I said, "when you told us those rules, there's one that you forgot."

"Which one was that?" he said through clenched teeth.

"Chill, dude."

GEORGE WASHINGTON IS MISSING!

★ ★ ★ ANNIE ★ ★ ★

A movie theater in the White House? It was amazing to think about.

When my family came from Poland to the United States, we had no friends. So, what did we do? We went to movies! It was fun, and there was English to learn. You like the way I talk? You can thank the movie stars.

At the movies, I watched and dreamed. But in all my wonderful dreams, I never thought of a movie theater in my own house! That Mr. President is a lucky man.

Mr. Flower showed us around the White House. As I watched him, I thought of my father. Mr. Flower acted strict, but his eyes were soft and warm.

He said, "For recreation, the White House has a variety of facilities. Besides the movie theater, it has a swimming pool and a bowling alley. There is also a tennis court—"

The girl named Dee gasped. "A tennis court? I want one of those!"

"—and a basketball court."

"All right!" said the boy named José. He spun around and did a motion that looked like dribbling a basketball.

I watched him and said to Dee, "He is a good mover."

She snorted. "Looks to me like he eats too much sugar at his house."

"What do you know about my house?" José asked her.

"Nothing."

He nodded. "That's right, nothing."

I wondered what they might say about my house. My family lives in Kansas City, Missouri. It is very different from Poland. My father was a chemist, but now he drives a taxi. My mother was a schoolteacher, and now she washes towels at the Hilton Hotel. There are lots of bathrooms at the Hilton Hotel. I work very hard to make my parents proud and to make my room feel like home. I have a picture of my grandmother. I also have posters of movie stars. But there is no movie theater.

Ms. Letter said, "Now, children, of all the beautiful things in this house, there is one item that's the most valuable. Do you know what it is?"

We looked at each other. No one knew.

"Answer the teacher!" said Mr. Flower.

Dee raised her hand. "The First Lady's fancy dresses?"

I said, "Maps?"

José guessed, "The president's flat-screen TV?"

"Wrong!" said Mr. Flower.

Ms. Letter told us, "Since you can't guess the most valuable item in the White House, I'll show it to you. Follow me, children, to the East Room."

She and Mr. Flower led us into a giant room that had beautiful decorations and a very high ceiling.

"And here we are, in the East Room!" said Ms. Letter. "This room has been used for celebrations and solemn events. But on a daily basis, it holds the most valuable item in the entire house."

She pointed to a painting that hung on the wall. Mr. Flower warned us, "Look, but don't touch!"

The painting showed a man in a fancy, old-fashioned

uniform. He seemed familiar. José stepped closer and gave a big smile. "Hey, I recognize him. It's the dude on my one-dollar bill!"

Dee turned up her nose. "I wouldn't know. The smallest bills I carry are five dollars."

I had no money. But I did have something else. I reached into my purse and showed it to them. "Here is my Kansas City bus pass!"

Ms. Letter was too excited to notice. "This is the portrait of our founding father, president of the United States, and first commander in chief, George Washington!"

Dee checked the painting. "Wow, he sure looks . . . not hot. Is that a wig?"

I told her, "My book says that he powdered his real hair."

She sighed. "No offense, but if this picture is the highlight of the tour . . ."

Dee looked at me. I looked at José. All of us said it together. "Bor-ing!"

"So," said Ms. Letter, "take a minute to connect with this famous painting, General George Washington welcoming us to the house where we all belong."

Mr. Flower looked at his watch. "You've got sixty seconds. Fifty-nine. Fifty-eight . . ."

José, Dee, and I walked up close to George Washington. I wondered what it would be like to powder my hair.

José shook his head. "Nothing personal, George, but I don't belong here."

"What do you mean?" asked Dee.

"Look around. Do you see any kids?"

"My book says many, many children have lived here," I told him.

José did one of his moves. "But were the kids anything like me?"

Dee rolled her eyes. "I think very few people on this planet are like you."

"I'm serious," said José. "Do you think any of these fancy schmancy presidential kids are for real? They eat off delicate dishes."

"And fly in helicopters," said Dee.

I glanced around the room. "And they live here, in this big, fancy house!"

"Kids like us are for real," said Dee.

"Kids like us have to study hard," said José.

"Kids like us don't have it easy," I said.

The three of us looked at one another. We didn't say it, but I knew we were all thinking the same thing: We don't belong here!

Mr. Flower looked at his watch and shouted, "Time's up! Everyone, this way!"

He and Ms. Letter led the group into the next room, leaving the three of us alone. When I started to follow, I bumped José. He fell against Dee. All of us knocked into the painting.

It fell down with a crash!

"Oops," said José.

Dee hissed, "José, what did you do?"

"Me? It was you!"

The painting lay face-down on the floor.

I said, *"Nie wierzyc wlasnym oczom!"*

Oh, sorry. Those are Polish words for "I cannot believe this!"

Dee shook her head. "We broke the most valuable thing in the White House. Now none of us will be able to run for office!"

"Or see our families again!" said José.

Dee turned to us. "Please, you guys, help me get it back up."

Together we reached down, lifted the painting, and leaned it against the wall. When we looked at it, Dee gasped. "Oh, no!"

"The One-Dollar Dude!" exclaimed José.

"O moj Boze!" I said. That means "Oh, my gosh!"

The painting was fine. It had no damage. There was just one problem.

In the picture George Washington was missing!

CAN YOU SAY LOST?

★ ★ ★ DEE ★ ★ ★

Okay, this place was creeping me out. It was bad enough that we couldn't turn on our cell phones or use the tennis court. But disappearing pictures?

This just in: The White House is haunted!

"Holy Potomac!" someone exclaimed.

I nodded. "You can say that again."

Then I looked at José. "Wait a minute. Did you say that?"

"Uh, no."

Annie shivered. "I did not either."

"Then who did?" I asked.

We glanced nervously at each other, then slowly turned around.

Standing in front of us was George Washington. He was posed just like in the painting, but he was real!

"Does anyone know how long I've stood like this?" he asked.

"A long time," said José, staring.

"A very long time," I added.

"More than two hundred years," said Annie.

Washington stretched and grunted. "That explains it. I thought I was feeling a little stiff."

He was standing in the room with us, but we still didn't believe it.

Annie said, "You are the person in the painting!"

José did a couple of moves that looked like Washington's poses. "You look like this on the dollar bill . . . and this on the quarter."

I added, "My mom bought me a really cool pair of jeans on your birthday."

Washington smiled. "How festive!"

I'd never seen a picture of him smiling. He looked goofy but nice. I told him, "You should smile more often."

"Let's make an agreement," he said. "I'll smile more if you do something for me."

"What's that?" I asked.

"Treat me like a normal person. I really am, you know."

Annie said, "A normal person? Oh, sir, we could not do that."

He sighed. "When people are around me, they're so stiff and proper. Sometimes I want to just, you know . . . relax. Take it easy."

José gave a hoot. "Get down, Mr. President! You the man!"

He shrugged. "The man? Well, I suppose I'm one of them."

Washington looked friendly and a little bit sad. Okay, he was the president, but to me he seemed like . . . well, a *George*. Later, when I talked to Anna and José, they said the same thing. All of us thought of him as George, but of course we would never call him that to his face.

I turned to George. "Tell us, Mr. President, how did it feel to stand in that pose for such a long time?"

"It was difficult," he said. "I stood in that frame every day and every night, in the summer and in the winter, even when my nose itched! I did it because, although I never spent a night in this building, I believe this house belongs to everyone. These walls don't just talk—they shout! My pose was a gesture of hospitality, welcoming one and all into the nation's home—your home, where all of you belong. You do feel that you belong, don't you?"

We looked at each other, then back at him. "No," said Annie.

Now it was George's turn to stare. "You don't? Why not?"

Annie said, "It's so big."

I said, "It's so old."

José said, "It's so . . . educational."

George stretched out his arms, as if he were trying to give the place a hug. "Do you know how much thought went into building this house? It's perfect!"

Annie glanced around. "The White House, it's beautiful, but . . ."

José jumped in. "It's like a party we haven't been invited to."

"A party?" said George, perking up. "I love parties. Let's find one, shall we?"

As he spoke Ms. Letter came flouncing into the room, leading the tour group. George quickly went back into his pose. We struck poses too, trying to stand perfectly still.

"Children of today," Ms. Letter was asking the group, "weren't the scalloped saucers absolutely fantastic? And how about those fabulous flora and fauna salad plates?"

As they moved into the next room Mr. Flower looked around. "Those missing kids—they have to be around here somewhere."

Searching the place, he walked right past us! Unfortunately, I was just thinking about George and how his nose had itched. Sure enough, mine starting itching too. There was no stopping it.

I sneezed!

"Bless you," said George.

Mr. Flower stopped and stared at him. "General George Washington?"

George decided to try out one of his smiles. "Hey, I like smiling," he told me. "It feels good."

"Sir, it really is you!" exclaimed Mr. Flower.

"At ease, soldier," said George.

Mr. Flower cleared his throat. "Pardon me for asking, sir, but why aren't you in your frame?"

George said, "I am inviting my befuddled children on a very special tour of the White House, so they relish its perfection and learn to feel comfortable here."

"Speaking of comfortable . . ." said José. He dropped his pose with a sigh of relief. So did Annie and I.

"Sir, did you say *your* children?" asked Mr. Flower, glancing at us. "I didn't know you had any."

George shrugged. "It's a metaphor. I'm their founding father."

"Well," said Mr. Flower, "'your' children are out of control. They left the tour. They broke rank. They disobeyed orders. Children of today—come with me! You are busted!"

Busted? In the White House? When my parents found out, I would be so grounded.

Just then, George pointed across the room. "Oh, look. The pastry chef!"

Mr. Flower whirled around. "Where?"

"Run!" George told us.

He tore out of the room. For an old guy, he sure could go fast!

"This way!" he yelled.

We followed him around a corner and down a hall, through three or four different rooms. The place was like one of those mazes, where you try to get out and can't. The good news was that Mr. Flower didn't know where we were. The bad news was that we didn't either.

Can you say lost?

PARTY!

★ ★ ★ JOSÉ ★ ★ ★

Dude, have you ever been lost?

I got lost at the mall once. It was scary. It felt like forever until my mom came back. I kept thinking, "What if nobody finds me and I have to live at Sears for the rest of my life?"

Where was George? He'd been with us a second ago, then he was gone. I watched Annie and Dee. They seemed scared too, the way I had felt that day at the mall.

I said, "Hey, where did he go? What do we do now?"

We looked around. There was no sign of him.

Then someone yelled, "Party!"

It was George. He came around a corner, holding a

handful of chips. "You've got to try the crab dip!" he exclaimed.

I said, "Mr. President, man, what are you talking about?"

"It tastes like sour cream," he said. "Plus something else. I don't know—dill?"

"Sir," said Annie, "where are you taking us? We don't know where we are."

George looked surprised. "You don't? Well, then come with me and I'll show you."

He led us down a hall, past room after room. As we walked, it was as if we were going back in time. In each room people were celebrating. There were elegant balls, Christmas tree lightings, pumpkin carvings.

"Whoa," I said. "We found a party."

"Lots of parties!" said Annie. She opened her notebook and wrote it down.

We kept going, past birthday celebrations, family get-togethers, and the White House Easter Egg Roll. Suddenly we saw a flash, and over our heads a disco ball sparkled and turned. There was thumping music and a big crowd.

I turned to George. "Mr. President, what is this?"

He answered, "A dance of some kind?"

Dee said, "It's a high school prom! But in the White House?"

As we stared at the crowd a girl came toward us. She had blond hair and was smiling. It seemed like she was looking at me, so I smiled back.

"Far out!" she said. "Welcome!"

She did a little dance move to the music. I did one right back. Hey, this girl was all right!

I said, "My name is José. Do I know you?"

"I'm Susan, silly!" she said. "You know, President Ford's daughter? You crack me up! Can you believe my dad let us have our high school prom here in the East Room? This is so much better than the school gym."

"Less smelly, for sure," said Dee.

Annie said, "Wait one minute, please." She looked in her book, and her eyebrows shot up. "President Ford? It says here that he was in White House from 1974 to 1977."

Susan jumped in the air, like a cheerleader. "Go, class of '75!"

George did a little jump of his own. I thought it was pretty good for an old dude. He yelled, "Let's hear it for 1975! And while we're at it, how about a cheer for 1775? Go, rebels!"

Susan said, "Did he say 1775? Wow, he's George Washington, isn't he? Just think, the first president at my

prom! This is so cool!" She walked around him, looking at his outfit. "Whatever it is that you're wearing, I love it!"

While Susan looked at George, Dee looked at Susan.

Dee said, "Your prom dress is so . . . retro."

Susan said, "Thanks—I think."

Annie was watching her too. "You are so beautiful, like a princess. Like a shining star."

I pictured Susan in a stretch limo, the kind that carries rock stars. She was in the backseat watching TV, and I was with her. I imagined us going through our family car wash. Did I tell you we offer a special deal for limos? You get a free wax with every wash. Check it out, man.

Susan shook her head sadly. "Can I tell you a secret? I'm not a princess, not even close. The truth is, it's not easy being the president's daughter."

"Not easy?" said Dee. "Look at this place. It's like a palace!"

Susan said, "It's more like a fish bowl. People are always watching. You can never stop smiling. Sometimes it seems like I have everything—except privacy."

"Come on," I said, "how bad can it be? If you want something, you just tell the secret service to get it, right?"

She laughed. "That's not the way it works. I have chores, like you do. I even have homework."

Homework? The sound of that word made my blood run cold.

Someone called, and Susan glanced over her shoulder. "I'd better be getting back. It was great meeting you. Enjoy the party!"

She headed off into the crowd. I was about to wade in and do a few dance moves, when we heard a familiar voice. "Hold it right there!"

It was Mr. Flower. He had found us.

"Uh-oh," said Dee.

He hurried toward us, yelling, "This is the White House, not a disco!"

George shot us a grin. "Time to go. Charge!"

We ran off in the other direction, past the lights and the crowd. Soon the music faded.

"That was fun!" said Dee.

"The party's over?" I asked.

"I guess so," said Annie.

George told us, "You must admit, it was festive and it was welcoming."

"True that!" I said.

He led us down a staircase and past more rooms, only these rooms didn't have parties. They had animals!

"Look at all of them!" said Annie. "Dogs, cats, raccoons and roosters, birds . . ."

Dee added, "A bear cub, a pig, a goat, a rabbit, a donkey . . ."

"There's a squirrel," I said.

"Oh, yes," said Annie, checking her book. "Pete the Squirrel, from 1922. And look what it says here: One president, he loved the animals so much, he fed the mice in the walls!"

"Yuck!" said Dee.

Suddenly I stopped in my tracks. "Dude, that's nothing compared to this."

"What do you mean?" asked Dee. She and Annie joined me at a window. We looked outside to the White House lawn.

I said, "Now, that's what I call a pet."

We were staring at an elephant.

RESTORING THE PAST

★ ★ ★ ANNIE ★ ★ ★

An elephant at the White House? I could not believe my eyes!

I looked in my book, and there I found the answer. I said proudly, "This elephant was a gift for President Dwight D. Eisenhower."

"Must be nice," said José. "My apartment building won't even let us have a fish tank."

Dee exclaimed, "And look, there's a hippo!"

"A *pigmy* hippo," I said, copying the information into my notebook. "That was from the Calvin Coolidge administration. It says here that when presidents got exotic pets as gifts, the animals were taken to the National Zoo."

"Children, keep moving," George told us. "To the right!"

He took us through a doorway, taking us back in time again. I glanced around. "Where are we? *When* are we?"

"We're in the Oval Office," George said. "I'm told that this was the first one, built in 1909. That desk is where the president works."

The desk was very beautiful. I wondered what it would be like to sit there and write in my notebook.

Just then a woman spoke from the next room. ". . . eight, nine, ten. Ready or not, here I come!"

A beautiful lady hurried into the Oval Office, wearing a little hat that was shaped like a box for pills. She gave us a funny look. "Oh! Who are you? What are you doing here?"

Then she saw George. "Mr. President? George Washington? Is that you?"

"Y-yes," he stuttered. "I don't believe we've had the pleasure!"

She said, "I am Jacqueline Kennedy, wife of John F. Kennedy, thirty-fifth president of the United States."

"Charmed!" said George. "And isn't that a delightful hat you're wearing. I wonder how it would look on my wife, Martha."

"She would be lovely, I am sure." Mrs. Kennedy checked the room. "Have you seen my daughter, Caroline? We were playing hide-and-seek."

"Boo!" said someone from behind the desk. A little girl came out. "Here I am, Mommy."

Can I tell you a secret? Sometimes I wish I had a sister. If I did, I would want her to be like this little girl.

"Caroline," said Mrs. Kennedy, "we have to go feed Macaroni."

"Macaroni?" asked Dee. "I love macaroni!"

"Me too," I said. "I like pasta."

José grinned. "Spaghetti rocks!"

Caroline looked at us and burst out laughing. "No, silly. Macaroni is the name of my pony!"

"You have a pony?" I asked.

She jumped up and down with excitement. "Yes, and I just got a lollipop!"

George said, "Where is your father, little one?"

Caroline smiled. "Oh, he's upstairs with his shoes and socks off. Not doing anything."

Mrs. Kennedy leaned over and kissed her daughter. "Sweetheart, see if your brother is up from his nap. Maybe your daddy can take the two of you to feed Macaroni and go for a ride."

"Yea!" said Caroline, and she ran out of the office.

Mrs. Kennedy went over to a table and picked up a file that was full of papers. She looked through it, then turned to George. "Mr. President, I have so wanted to talk with you about the White House. We're restoring it, you know."

George blushed. "Well, my dear, I did select the original design myself. But then, I suppose you know that."

"Yes, that's what I've read," said Mrs. Kennedy. "Honestly, though, the problem isn't so much your original design. It's what the other presidents added—or took away. We're working from the inside out, bringing back the White House you originally planned and setting it up for the future, creating spaces to live and work, making it a place that all Americans can be proud of."

As she spoke, a man came into the room, pushing a desk. His suit was old-fashioned.

"Excuse me, sir," said Mrs. Kennedy. "May I help you?"

He stopped and wiped off his forehead. "I'm President Martin Van Buren."

José leaned over to Dee and whispered, "That guy's a president? He sure looks old!"

"The desk looks really old too," said Dee.

"Oh, Mr. President," said Mrs. Kennedy, "where are you taking that desk?"

"I don't like it, and I want new drapes," he said.

"Congress won't give me more money, so I'm going to sell this at a yard sale. Everyone loves a yard sale!"

"Not everyone," said Mrs. Kennedy. "If you ask me, the White House has had far too many yard sales—or worse. At some point presidential china ended up in the Potomac River!"

She turned back to President Van Buren. "Sir, that's an important piece of furniture. Don't you realize how historically valuable it is?"

I tried to help her. "Yes, sir," I told him. "That is an antique."

He said, "To you it may be an antique. To me it's clutter. What's my family supposed to do with all this stuff?"

Mrs. Kennedy stood up, strong and proud. "It belongs to the American people. We do not sell historical pieces. And we do not throw presidential china in the river. Now please, take that back!"

He shrugged. "Yes, ma'am. I'll just put this in the library."

As President Van Buren left, we heard music from above us. There was a crash, and piano legs stuck through the ceiling!

"Oh, dear," said Mrs. Kennedy. "That's Margaret Truman's piano. It came through the ceiling in 1948.

That's one reason why her father, President Harry Truman, decided to rebuild the White House interior."

Mrs. Kennedy opened her file and made some notes. "I'll take care of it. We'll fix the ceiling, then the piano."

She looked up at us, her eyes shining. "The way I see it, I'm not just restoring a house or some furniture. I'm restoring our past, so we can build the future. Think of all the history these walls have seen! If we don't listen, then we'll never learn from the past."

Mrs. Kennedy reached into her file and held up two bits of fabric. "And now, I need your help! I've been working to restore the Oval Office, and I'm trying to decide between these two. Which fabric would better serve the spirit of this room? Let's have a vote."

She held up one fabric. "All those in favor of this one?"

George and José shrugged and raised their hands.

"Thank you," said Mrs. Kennedy. She held up the other fabric. "Those in favor of this one?"

Dee and I liked that one best, so we raised our hands. Mrs. Kennedy raised hers, too.

"I agree," she said. "Since this is a democracy, and majority rules . . ."

I could see that something was bothering George. He whispered to José, "Young man, why are the women voting?"

Mrs. Kennedy heard him. "Ah, sir, you may not have heard that women won the right to vote in 1920. It became a constitutional amendment."

George nodded his head slowly. "That's fascinating. Women voting. Why didn't I think of that?"

"Then it's decided!" said Mrs. Kennedy.

Dee gave her a big grin. "Restoration—hey, I like this idea!"

José nodded. "I hope my mom never gets rid of the La-Z-Boy in our den. She says that chair was the only thing that would rock me to sleep when I was a baby."

I said, "We have a painting of a mountain with yellow flowers that my father bring from the old country. Sometimes he forget that it's there. Some days I see him look at it a lot."

George looked off into the distance. "When I was a child, my father carved me a sturdy rocking horse so I could play soldier. I kept that toy, hoping I would give it to my child one day. I wonder where it is now."

Mrs. Kennedy put away the fabric and closed the file. "Perhaps the four of you would enjoy walking upstairs and seeing the renovations we have done to Lincoln's bedroom?"

"Lincoln?" said George.

"President Abraham Lincoln," I explained. "He was president before Mr. Kennedy."

George sighed. "Weren't we all?"

He looked sad. I wondered what it was like to be father of a whole country. It sounded to me like a hard job.

I offered him my arm. He took it. As we followed Mrs. Kennedy out of the Oval Office, I decided that now I had two fathers, and I was glad.

7

GLORIOUS GLASS

★ ★ ★ DEE ★ ★ ★

Okay, I admit it. I didn't turn off my cell phone.

We were heading down a hall behind Mrs. Kennedy, when all of a sudden the phone started beeping in my pocket. As I fumbled for it, someone yelled from behind me.

"No cell phones!"

It was Mr. Flower. He had found us again.

"Okay, okay," I said. "You don't have to shout."

I clicked off the phone. But he wasn't done. He walked over to George, shaking his head.

"This is it, sir. I really must insist. The next tour will be arriving any minute, and you are not in your right frame . . . of mind."

George said, "You're relentless, Mr. Flower. And you make bad puns."

"I mean it, sir. You belong in the picture frame, and these kids belong with their tour."

"Mr. Flower, man, we'd like to help you," said José, nodding at the rest of us, "but we joined another tour."

"That is correct," said Annie. "We are now on the proud tour of Mrs. Jacqueline Kennedy."

Mr. Flower grunted. "Jackie Kennedy? Yeah, right."

I looked around. Mrs. Kennedy was gone!

"She was here just a minute ago," I said.

"Nice try, kids," said Mr. Flower. "Now, let's move it."

George winked at us. "I have just one thing to say about that."

"What is it?" asked Mr. Flower.

"Run!" shouted George.

We raced off down the hallway. Rooms flashed by as we went. Once again, we were going back in time. This was the kind of tour I liked!

I said, "Look, an indoor pool!"

"Let's dive in!" said José.

Annie said, "I love to swim!"

Mr. Flower was behind us, trying to keep up. He yelled, "Stop!"

"Why?" said George. "The water looks so inviting."

"Is it dangerous?" asked Annie.

"Is it deep?" asked José.

I don't know why, but I laughed. "Are there sharks?" I asked.

"Yes!" said Mr. Flower.

We stared at him.

"Especially," he added, "since the pool got changed to the Press Room in the 1970s."

Was it possible? Did Mr. Flower make a joke?

A door opened, and suddenly we were back in the present. Ms. Letter walked in with her tour group. George ducked into a side room so Ms. Letter wouldn't see him. She droned on as if nothing had happened. "Children of today, at the turn of the twentieth century the world-famous artist Louis Comfort Tiffany created a beautiful stained-glass screen for the White House. It's no longer here, but you can imagine how lovely it must have been."

As we gazed at the place where Ms. Letter was pointing, the room began to glow. Colors appeared—reds, yellows, brilliant blues. I could hardly believe my eyes. It was the Tiffany screen!

Annie gasped. "So beautiful."

"Wow!" said José.

I said, "It's like a dream."

"Wow!" said José.

George said, "Blessed Chesapeake Bay, this is glorious glass."

"Wow!" said José.

"Uh, José," I said, "are you all right?"

"I'm cool." He moved up close and studied the patterns. "I wish we had one of these at our car wash. The customers could look at it while they were waiting."

Mr. Flower had been standing off to the side, trying to restrain himself. Finally he couldn't stand it anymore. "What are you kids looking at? The glass is gone."

Ms. Letter said, "He's right. It doesn't exist anymore."

José asked, "What happened to it?"

"President Theodore Roosevelt had it torn down."

"See?" said Mr. Flower. "What did I tell you?"

He crossed his arms and leaned against the wall. There was the sound of breaking glass!

"Huh?" said Mr. Flower. "What happened?"

Ms. Letter clapped her hands to get the group's attention. "Children of today," she said. "Let's go visit the West Wing."

As she led them away, we hung back. A moment later George appeared in a doorway. "Mrs. Kennedy said Lincoln's bedroom is upstairs," he told us. "Shall we go find it?"

He moved off, and we followed. Behind us I heard Mr. Flower mumbling, "What was that noise? Where am I? Where is everyone? This reminds me of the time I was lost at Sears."

We climbed the stairs, going back in time, and found our way to Lincoln's bedroom. It didn't look like my room at home. In fact, it didn't look like any bedroom I'd ever seen.

"This can't be Lincoln's bedroom," said José. "There's no bed!"

Annie checked her book. "It says here that in Lincoln's time, this room was his office."

"Looks like he's been writing," I said, noticing a pen and paper.

There was the sound of footsteps. George whispered, "Someone is coming!"

I looked around and spotted a closet. It would be a perfect place to hide. Plus, maybe we would find some shoes!

"Over there!" I said.

We piled inside, only to find that someone had beaten us to it. He was a boy our age, dressed in old-time clothes.

Annie stared at him. "Who are you?"

"I'm Tad. I like to hide in my pa's closet."

"Well, move over, dude," said José. "You're not the only one who wants to hide."

I pulled the door toward us, keeping it open a crack so we could see out. As we watched, a bearded man wearing a black suit walked into the room.

"He looks familiar," I said.

José perked up. "That's the dude on the five-dollar bill! It's Abraham Lincoln!"

I glanced over at Tad. "So that means . . . you're his son?"

Tad grinned and nodded. As we watched, a woman entered the room with Lincoln.

"That's my ma," said Tad.

"He is right," said Annie, showing us her book. "See? Mary Todd Lincoln. Here is her picture."

"Hey," said Tad, "you want to go up in the attic and ring all the bells? It makes everyone run around like there's an emergency!"

I smiled. Tad might be wearing old-fashioned clothes, but he could have been one of the kids in my neighborhood. As I watched President and Mrs. Lincoln, though, my smile faded. They looked worried.

"We don't have to ring the bells," I said. "I think something urgent is already going on."

Annie gasped. "Of course! The Civil War!"

I WAS THERE

★ ★ ★ JOSÉ ★ ★ ★

Dude, being crowded together in that closet, it reminded me of home! I missed my mom, my aunt, my uncle. I even missed my brother—well, almost.

Tad must have read my mind. "I have a brother," he said sadly. "His name is Willie, and he's very sick."

Dee gave him a funny look. "But you're the president's kids. You guys must have good health care."

As she spoke, President Lincoln turned to his wife. "I don't see that there's any other choice."

Mrs. Lincoln said, "This proclamation that you're planning—have you thought through all the consequences?"

He put his arm around her shoulders and said in a gentle voice, "It's impossible to know all the consequences."

Mrs. Lincoln shivered. "Soldiers were at our door, trying to get in out of the cold."

"And what did you do?" he asked.

"What could I do? Forty men are sleeping in the East Room."

That surprised me. I leaned over to Tad. "You have soldiers camping out in the White House?"

Tad nodded. "Some of them are wounded."

"War is hard," said Annie. "My grandmother told me it changed the old country so much."

George nodded. It looked like he was remembering hard times of his own.

Mrs. Lincoln said, "I'm worried, Abraham. Some people say your proclamation will bring deeper division and more bloodshed."

"I pray it isn't true," he answered.

I could see she wasn't happy with his answer. The look on her face reminded me of my mom, when she makes up her mind about something.

Mrs. Lincoln said, "We need more than prayers. Willie is ill. And I worry about you, about our family. The death threats—"

"Our Willie will get better," said President Lincoln. "He's a strong boy."

She said, "He needs to go where it's warmer—to my sister's, down south."

"That isn't possible. It's not safe."

"It's not safe here either!" she exclaimed.

"You know what I mean," said President Lincoln.

"Forget the nation," she said. "This is our family!"

Mrs. Lincoln started to cry. I was surprised. In my family we don't cry very much.

President Lincoln put his arms around her. After a minute, she looked up at him. "Abraham, slavery has been a way of life for so long. How much sacrifice will it take to change that?"

He told her, "I don't know."

"God help us," said Mrs. Lincoln. She wiped her eyes, kissed him on the cheek, and left the room.

The light changed, and I could tell that time had passed. President Lincoln looked older. He walked around the room, then went over and sat at his desk, where there was a sheet of paper. Studying the paper, he sighed and buried his head in his hands. I tell you, man, it surprised me. When I see the president on TV, he always looks good—you know, strong, in control.

I didn't know presidents got tired or sad.

Next to me George said, "Slavery is a terrible thing."

"Did you have slaves?" Dee asked him.

"I set all my slaves free when I died."

"Do you think owning slaves was wrong?" she asked.

Before he could answer, Tad brushed past us. I tried to stop him, but he opened the door and went to his father.

"Pa . . ."

"Tad?" said Lincoln, looking up. "Why are you still awake?"

"I couldn't sleep. Are you mad at me?"

"No, son. Recently I've had trouble sleeping too."

Tad climbed onto his father's lap. "Pa, I was proud that you were elected president. But sometimes I wish it had never happened."

"I can understand that."

Tad said, "Ma's worried. She cries a lot."

"I know. But everything will be all right."

That seemed to make Tad angry. "If it's all right, then why are you and Ma and everyone fighting?"

"Your mother and I—"

"Why do people say you're dividing the country? And why are the soldiers allowed to wear their muddy boots in the house when I can't?"

"Because—"

"Pa," said Tad, "why are you making new house rules?"

Lincoln looked down at his son. He thought for a moment. Then he said, "Because black hands helped build this White House."

Tad said, "Well, maybe we should go live somewhere else."

"Or," said his father, "maybe we should let everyone live free."

Lincoln gave Tad a hug. It made me feel better. I hated to see them argue. "Now, get along to bed, young man."

"Good night, Pa," said Tad.

"Good night, Tadpole," said Lincoln.

When his son was gone, Lincoln went back to the desk, murmuring, "If my hand trembles when I sign it, they will say I was unsure." He gazed down at the paper, then turned, walked across the room, and looked out the window.

Annie looked over at me. "What is Mr. Lincoln talking about?"

"I don't know," I said. "What's that paper he's deciding to sign?"

"There's one way to find out," said Dee. She opened

the closet door and tiptoed to the desk. Annie and I went with her, while George hung back.

Dee picked up the paper and read, "'By the President of the United States of America: A Proclamation. . . . All persons held as slaves within any State or designated part of a State, the people whereof shall then be in rebellion against the United States, shall be then, thenceforward, and forever free.'"

She looked up from the paper. "Guys, it's the Emancipation Proclamation!"

Lincoln must have heard her. When he turned around, he saw us standing by the desk. He could have called the guards. Instead he asked, "Who are you?"

I tried to smile. I'm not sure it worked. "Sir, my name is José. This is Annie and Dee."

He cocked his head and studied us. "Do I know you?"

There was something about his expression that made me feel strong. "Maybe you do," I said.

Annie stepped up beside me. "Mr. Lincoln, you must sign this paper."

Dee said, "It's for me. It's for us, all of us."

"We are the future," said Annie. "We are America."

"Sir," I told him, "some of us look different. Some of

us speak with an accent. But we love our country."

Annie said, "My mother tells me that freedom must start someplace. Sir, I think this is the place. This is the first step."

"Please, sign the paper," said Dee. "You can change the world. It can start with you."

As Dee spoke, George stepped out from the shadows. He crossed the room and walked up to Lincoln. At first Lincoln was surprised. Then he smiled and nodded.

"Mr. President," said Lincoln.

"Mr. President," said George.

George reached down, picked up the pen, and handed it to Lincoln. Lincoln weighed it in his palm. Then he looked at us and said, "Never in my life have I felt more certain that I was doing right. My hand will not waver. My signature must be steady."

Leaning over the desk, he signed the paper. The world changed. I was there.

YOU'RE HISTORY!

★ ★ ★ ANNIE ★ ★ ★

"The British are coming!"

Was this the famous Paul Revere, calling his warning in Boston? No! It was a lady in the White House. She came running into the State Dining Room after we left President Lincoln. It was another place and another time.

George recognized this lady. "Mrs. Madison? Mrs. Dolley Madison, my old friend!"

"Who's she?" asked Dee.

I read from my book, then wrote it in my notebook. "Dolley Madison is First Lady to James Madison, fourth president of the United States."

"President Washington," said Mrs. Madison, trying

to catch her breath, "I need your help! The British are coming! They're going to burn down the house!"

George scratched his head. "The British? But we already defeated them in the Revolutionary War!"

Dee said, "I guess this is another war!"

"Another war?" asked Washington.

José shook his head sadly. "Dude, so many wars."

"The book says it is the War of 1812," I told them.

Mrs. Madison nodded. "President Madison is away, fighting at the front, and everything will turn to ashes! This beautiful house will be destroyed!"

José looked around nervously. "Maybe we should get out of here."

"Mrs. Madison," said George, "you and the children must leave. The house is not safe."

Mrs. Madison shook her head. Her face was kind but determined. "No, I can't leave yet. I must save the most important item in the entire house. That's why I came to the State Dining Room."

The most important item? I wondered what it was. Then I remembered. Mrs. Madison was talking about the painting!

"Please, Mrs. Madison, just go," begged George.

"But your portrait, I must save it!" she said. "It's what I'm remembered for!"

José glanced over at us. "She's right. We can't leave that behind."

"We can't let President Washington burn to ashes!" I added.

"Yes, you can!" said George. "I'm just oil paint and canvas."

"You're valuable!" said Dee.

"You're art!" added José.

"You're history!" I told him.

We heard crashing and shouting outside. George looked worried.

"I command you all to leave!" he said.

Believe it or not, we didn't obey. Instead we listened to the lady with the strong voice. "Children, help me take down the painting!"

José rushed over and tried to remove it. "It won't budge. Someone bolted it down!"

Dee looked at George, with pleading in her eyes. "We can't get it off the wall. But we have to!"

"Who cares?" said George. "It's just a picture! And the British are getting closer!"

Dee and I tried to help José. It was no use. We had to leave the painting behind. It reminded me of all the things my family had left behind in Poland—big things, important things.

George led us outside. We stood beside him on the front lawn.

Next to me Dee took a gold pendant from around her neck and held it close to her. "If my house was on fire, I'd save this pendant, because it has a picture of my parents and me when I was a baby. If I didn't have the pendant, then I might not remember who I was."

José reached into his pocket and pulled out an old

coin made of silver. "My father gave this to my mom, who gave it to me. It's more than just money. It keeps me close to my family."

I tried to think of what I would save if my house was on fire. Suddenly I knew. "I would save this notebook," I told them. "It's special because I write down stories and thoughts in both languages. If I did not exist anymore, the notebook would let people know I was a real person. It's like the history . . . of me."

Just then a door opened and someone walked out of the White House. It was Dolley Madison. She was carrying something that was wrapped in a blanket.

"When my house was on fire," she told us, "this is what I saved."

Mrs. Madison unwrapped the blanket. The painting was inside!

MY HERO

Dolley Madison never owned a cell phone. She never had a lawn service or a fancy car. But she was my hero. I hurried over and gave her a big hug.

José grinned at her. "Dude, you did it! You saved the painting!"

I wondered, could a First Lady be a dude?

I gazed at the painting. It truly was beautiful. But it was still missing one thing—George Washington. He stood beside us, shaking his head in amazement. "Mrs. Madison, thank you for what you've done. But I'm not worth all this trouble."

"You built this country," I told him.

"And set up the framework for everything," added José.

"And now that frame is empty," said Annie.

George looked off into the distance. "I wanted to serve all the people of this nation. But now I see there are things I could have done when I had the chance."

Dee put her hand on his arm. "Building a country is hard work."

He said, "But my perfect home . . . is not perfect."

"My home, it is not perfect either," said Annie. "My parents love me, but they argue too much."

José shrugged. "My brother and I barely know our father."

"Sometimes I wish I had a brother and sister," I told him. "And more shoes."

"But you know what?" said Annie. "It still is home. My parents left our country because they want this to be *my* country."

"That's right," I said. "And my mom and dad vote in every election, because their voice counts."

"And people wait in line every day to come see your portrait," said José, "even when it's hot and muggy or really, really cold!"

"I don't understand," said George. "Why?"

Looking at Annie and José, I said, "Let's show him."

I walked over and stood in front of the painting. José stepped in next to me, and Annie lined up beside him.

I told George, "This is a new portrait."

"It is a picture of America," said Annie.

"Dude," said José, "you know why they spell it U.S.? Because it's us—all of us!" He did a little dance move and grinned.

Watching us, George threw his arms out wide. "Now this . . . this is a beautiful portrait!"

I said, "We're all here because of a home you helped to build, more than two hundred years ago."

Annie chimed in. "It's a good house."

George smiled at us. "Should you ever decide to run for office, you can count on my vote. And now, it's time for me to go back where I belong. I miss my painting and the wall where it hangs."

José nodded. "It would be nice to be a part of those walls."

As George stepped toward the painting, Annie cried out, "Wait! Don't leave without us!"

"I must," said George. "Duty calls."

Annie said, "Then at least take something to remember us by." Pulling out her notebook, she hugged it to her chest, then handed it to George. "I want you to have this."

I knew how important that notebook was to Annie. I had something important too. Reaching up around my neck, I unfastened the clasp on my pendant. Cupping the pendant gently in my hand, I gave it to George. "This is for you."

José shuffled his feet, then reached into his pocket and got his silver coin. "This is yours. Take it."

George handled the gifts carefully, lovingly. Then he gave us one last smile. "Thank you, all of you. It's been an honor to welcome you to the White House, a home where we all belong."

He tucked the gifts into his jacket, close to his heart, then resumed his pose and stepped back into the painting.

The light flickered. Suddenly, we were standing in the East Room, and the painting was back on the wall. Ms. Letter entered, leading our tour group.

"And, as I was saying, this wallpaper is magnificent! Don't you agree?"

The other kids nodded, looking bored. But to the three of us, the White House was anything but boring. It was a home—our home, and we couldn't wait to see more.

Just then a door flew open, and Mr. Flower came running in. Spotting us, he breathed a sigh of relief. "I found you! I thought I'd lost you, and my job, and my mind. But you are all here!"

José did a little dance step and said, "Don't forget the rule."

"What rule?" asked Mr. Flower.

"Chill, dude."

Then something amazing happened. Mr. Flower smiled! It was shaky, it was nervous, but it was definitely a smile.

"Security can make a person so insecure!" he said. "But I love this house. And I just want everyone to be safe. And sound. And happy, at home with George—uh, I mean, with President Washington."

Annie and José smiled. I could tell they felt the same way I did. When we first came to the White House, we had felt strange and out of place. Now we knew the truth. We belong. All of us belong.

I glanced over at the painting. George looked down on us, posing gravely. And then, could it have been my imagination?

George winked at us.

WHITE HOUSE

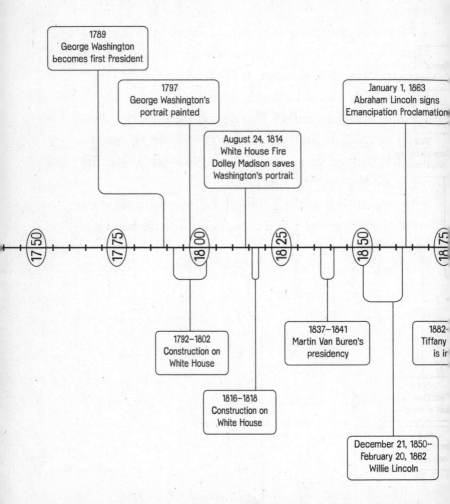

1789
George Washington becomes first President

1797
George Washington's portrait painted

August 24, 1814
White House Fire
Dolley Madison saves
Washington's portrait

January 1, 1863
Abraham Lincoln signs
Emancipation Proclamation

17 50   17 75   18 00   18 25   18 50   18 75

1792–1802
Construction on
White House

1816–1818
Construction on
White House

1837–1841
Martin Van Buren's
presidency

1882–
Tiffany
is ir

December 21, 1850–
February 20, 1862
Willie Lincoln

TiMELiNE

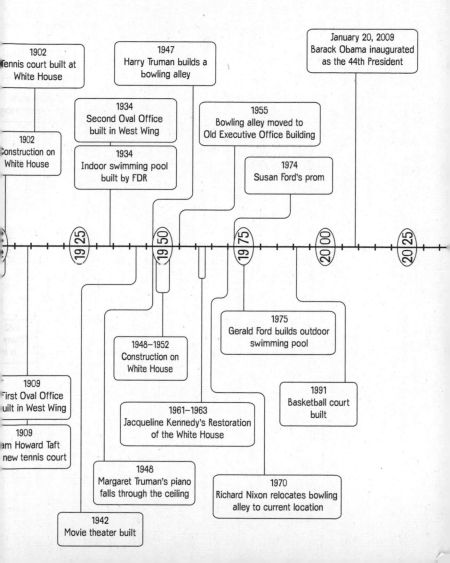

1902
Tennis court built at White House

1947
Harry Truman builds a bowling alley

January 20, 2009
Barack Obama inaugurated as the 44th President

1934
Second Oval Office built in West Wing

1955
Bowling alley moved to Old Executive Office Building

1902
Construction on White House

1934
Indoor swimming pool built by FDR

1974
Susan Ford's prom

1975
Gerald Ford builds outdoor swimming pool

1909
First Oval Office built in West Wing

1948–1952
Construction on White House

1991
Basketball court built

1909
William Howard Taft new tennis court

1961–1963
Jacqueline Kennedy's Restoration of the White House

1948
Margaret Truman's piano falls through the ceiling

1970
Richard Nixon relocates bowling alley to current location

1942
Movie theater built

19 25 19 50 19 75 20 00 20 25